Zeep Needs More Sleep

by Paul M. Kramer

Zeep Needs More Sleep by Paul M. Kramer

Aloha Publishers LLC
848 North Rainbow Boulevard, #4738
Las Vegas, NV 89107
www.alohapublishers.com

Inquiries, comments or further information are available at, www. alohapublishers.com.

Illustrations by Helga Tacke, helgatacke@yahoo.com.
Audio by Charly Espina Takahama charly@pmghawaii.com
Collaborator, Co-Editor, Cynthia Kress Kramer

This book is dedicated to Jennifer Kelley, Counselor and Mary Costales, Librarian, who have played an important role in enriching the lives of so many students at Makawao Elementary School located in Maui, Hawaii.

Jennifer made me aware that many of the students were not getting enough sleep which diminished their ability to concentrate and learn. She believed that a book that children could identify with about the importance of getting the right amount of sleep would be very beneficial and was very much needed. Mary Costales gave me the opportunity to visit the school and allowed me to read and talk to approximately one hundred of the school's first graders. That positive and enlightening experience was a stepping stone for my future plans to visit elementary schools throughout the country.

ISBN 13 (EAN): 978-0-9827596-0-8
Library of Congress Control Number (LCCN): 2010940360
Printed in Guangzhou, China. Production date: September 2014 Cohort: Batch 1

Zeep Needs More Sleep

by Paul M. Kramer

Aloha
PUBLISHERS
Books & Stories by Paul M. Kramer

Zeep's teacher said, "Going to bed too late makes it harder to learn and to be wise."

She also said, "A lack of sleep makes it more difficult to get out of bed and arise."

Zeep has difficulty waking up and repeatedly hits the snooze alarm to sleep five minutes more.

Zeep doesn't think clearly in the morning and has trouble getting out the door.

Did you know that getting less sleep makes it more difficult to pay attention and to learn?

Teachers say this is a big problem and is a cause for concern.

Zeep only goes to sleep when he cannot keep his eyes open anymore.

His parents tell him to go to bed, but their warnings he ignores.

Zeep frequently begs to stay up just a little while longer.

Do you think Zeep realizes that sleeping less makes it harder for him to grow bigger and stronger?

It is very important to get the proper amount of sleep each night.

Did you know that an extra hour of sleep can make the difference between being relaxed and calm rather than being uptight?

Have you ever insisted that you weren't tired or ready to go to sleep?

Not getting enough sleep could make you cranky which is what happens to Zeep.

Some of us are scared to go to sleep because we're afraid of the dark and being alone.

Knowing that our family is close by should give us the confidence to go to bed on our own.

About one hour before going to bed, Zeep's cousin Philippe gets tired.

Zeep has a bad habit of eating something sweet before going to bed and becomes wired.

Zeep sleeps eight hours compared to Philippe's ten hours per night.

Not getting enough sleep can affect someone's weight and height.

When Philippe gets up in the morning he is refreshed and ready to go.

Zeep doesn't want to get out of bed because his energy level is low.

Zeep and Philippe are cousins and are in the same grade.

Philippe is always alert and ready to learn while Zeep is moody and often afraid.

Many of us come up with excuses why we can't go to sleep.
Others look forward to going to sleep, like Philippe.
By not getting enough zzz's, many of us including Zeep get C's.
Philippe gets A's because he makes the most of his abilities.

Zeep and Philippe look forward to Saturday and Sunday.

They believe weekends were created to have fun and to play.

This past Saturday and Sunday was more special than others because it was the weekend of the County Fair.

The County Fair only comes to town once a year.

It seemed like just about everyone in town went to the County Fair.

Zeep and Philippe knew almost everybody there.

Philippe went on a scary roller coaster ride with his friend Jim.

Suddenly, Jim's safety belt broke, but luckily Philippe was sitting in back of Jim and was able to save him.

News spread quickly about Philippe saving Jim.

Philippe's courage and quick reflexes was the reason he was able to save him.

The Mayor of the town presented a gold medal to Philippe.

Philippe told everyone that he was able to react so quickly because he gets plenty of sleep.

THE DA

EXTRA

HERO

When asked about
...roic act,
...id;

The Mayor declared that the following week is to be named, "Get More Sleep Week."

The Mayor also stated that this special week be dedicated to our newest town hero, "Philippe."

Everyone in town tried to figure out several different ways to get more sleep.

Just about everyone was willing to give it a try and see how it worked for a week.

Zeep was proud of his cousin Philippe and was also willing to try sleeping more during this special week.

On the third day, one of his classmates said, "You look mighty cute today, Zeep."

Zeep was able to concentrate and pay more attention in class each day.

On the fifth day of "Get More Sleep Week", Zeep had a test in math and got an A.

After "Get More Sleep Week" was over, everyone realized they were better off than they were before.

Their lives had improved just by sleeping a minimum of one hour more.

Everyone was in a better mood and was as nice as could be.

Sleeping more helped Zeep and the entire community.

Are you willing to give it a try and go to sleep earlier

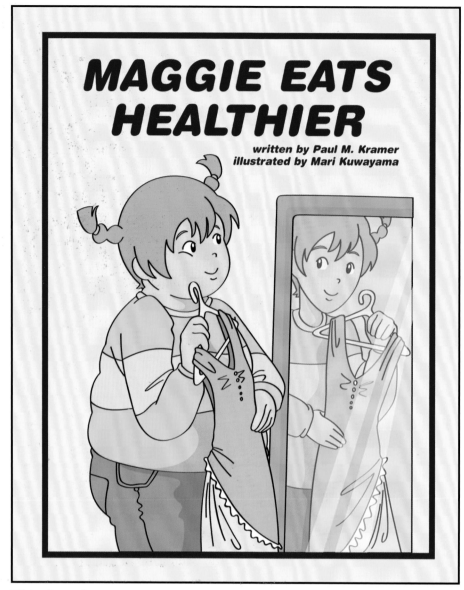

This is a heartwarming story about a 14 year old girl named Maggie who loved to play sports but found it difficult to reach her potential because of her weight issues. She changed her life by altering her eating habits and exercising regularly. As a result she became more physically fit and was able to achieve her goal of being the best she was capable of being. She also realized that nutritious foods could actually be quite tasty. Through time, regular exercise and better eating habits, Maggie's confidence improved and she was healthier and happier.

ISBN: 978-0-9827596-7-7, retail price: $15.95, size: 8" x 10"

Other Books Available by Paul M. Kramer

This story was written with the intent to motivate children to seek help when being bullied. Bullying is a very serious problem that has reached unacceptable and uncontrollable levels in recent years and must be dealt with.

Mikey was unwilling to be bullied any longer. Although Mikey was taking karate lessons to learn self-defense, he realized that fighting the bullies was not the best way to solve his problem. Instead, he found the courage to tell his teacher, which turned out to be the right thing to do and as a result the bullies were held accountable for their actions.

This is a must read for children and for the parents of young children who are having problems with bullies and bullying.

ISBN: 978-1-941095-14-0, retail price: $15.95, size: 8" x 10"

About the Author

Paul M. Kramer lives in Hawaii on the beautiful island of Maui with his wife Cindy and their son Lukas. Paul was born and raised in New York City.

Mr. Kramer's books attempt to reduce stress and anxiety and resolve important issues children face in their everyday lives. His books are often written in rhyme. They are entertaining, inspirational, educational and easy to read. One of his goals is to increase the child's sense of self worth.

He has written books on various subjects such as bullying, divorce, sleep deprivation, worrying, shyness, and weight issues.

Mr. Kramer has appeared on "Good Morning America," "The Doctors," "CNN Live" as well as several other Television Shows in the United States and Canada. He's been interviewed and aired on many radio programs including the British Broadcasting System and has had countless articles written about his work in major newspapers and magazines throughout the world.

More information about this book and Paul M. Kramer's other books are available on his website at www.alohapublishers.com.